# LATOYA LAWRENCE

## Secret Admirer

This book was professionally typeset on Reedsy.
Find out more at reedsy.com

# Contents

# Foreword

**Welcome To the Tantalizing Tales Collection: Toya's Titles of Terror, Treachery, And Suspense Shorties** *Volume Two*

In Volume two of this series two separate stories take place—the first a continuation from **Book one** that moves into its own tale of torture.

And the second, a standalone that moves in line with another one of its own quirks and craziness.

***Enjoy the out of the ordinary ride!***

# Preface

**Tale One:**

*Secret Admirer*

Bryce Brandon has found the love of his life—the only woman for him—but someone else is looking to take this lovely lady's place. Watching and waiting behind the scenes for the opportunity to snatch Bryce up for them self this mysterious individual will stop at nothing to get their hand on the object of their affections, and fervent desire—even if it causes them to kill for it!

**Tale Two:**

*The Dollhouse*

Lorna Ferguson is a twelve year old loner with a secret. A secret she likes to incorporate into her alone time play. The games in her life become real. The reality of her games become deadly.

This young girl does not play when it comes to others or those that cross her, so do not play with this little girl—if you do it may cause you your life!

viii

# Acknowledgments

A native of Queens, New York LaToya Lawrence is the author of thirteen previous titles:

Forgive Me Father (*Tantalizing Tales Volume One*), Inherent, The Session, The Bakery Boutique, The Backwater Summer Lake Resort, Lady, Fatal Beauty, New York Style Tales Of Suspense, God Has The Last Word, Wellness In Style, Harmonic Inspirations, Danielle's Diary, My Cup Overflows

# One

# The Sentencing

Judge Cedric Ambrose appeared from his chambers with a casefile in hand.

"*All rise,*" bailiff Asa O'Dell interjected to those seated in the courtroom.

Once the judge reached the bench the court officer addressed spectators in the gallery again.

"Court is now in session. You may take your seats."

Present this early morning during the sentencing of thirty-one-year-old former priest Kaiden Lucas aka *Father Asher Verlice* in the statutory rape and murder of seven high school catholic students six months ago was the families of the victims, and members of clergy and staff who served and taught at *Saint*

*Josephine Margaret Bakhita Preparatory, Parish,* and *Convent.*

Also present were friends of the families, neighbors of the community, and other public folk who had heard about the high publicized murder and scandal after the incidents hit the airwaves months back.

*Kaiden had pled guilty during his arraignment after his arrest.*

Brought out in handcuffs to meet with his attorney in front of the judge legal counsel tried to assert a mental instability pardon on behalf of his client.

Backing up his claim with a psychological evaluation by a criminal psychologist who assessed Kaiden to denote emotional scarring due to childhood abuse through trauma from peers at the root of his latter inappropriate, violent behavior he hoped for a persuasion of leniency in the judge's outcome.

Yalena Cordero Brown sat appalled at the motion made by the attorney as she sat beside her husband and two sons there in the tension-filled environment.

*What a weak, pathetic excuse. A plethora of people from all levels of society were teased or bullied during their youth yet did not ponder over it with pent up frustration throughout the years to eventually become ruthless sexual predators who killed in cold blood,* the woman infuriatingly ruminated.

"Alright," the honorable judge Cedric Ambrose said. "I have carefully reviewed and taken a considerable amount of time in my deliberation. I weighed over the facts and the circumstances of the events. I have also considered that the defendant has no prior criminal record or history of arrest. However, the nature of these crimes is reprehensible—especially for a man who took an oath and posed as a man of the cloth. You were supposed to illustrate someone for adults and children alike to look up to, to trust, to lead in faith, and to feel comfortable in seeking help from. Not someone to fear, deceive, abuse their position, and cause monstrous harm. You had a high moral and humane role of responsibility in which you failed tremendously. Your actions, Mr. Lucas, were deplorable and inexcusable—."

*Kaiden's attorney knew the bleak direction in where the judge started to head. A chance for mercy seemed out of the question right about now.*

The man of counsel sighed warily, inside, doing all that he priorly could for his client to receive a reduced prison sentence that did not appear probable. He tried one last appeal to the court on behalf of Kaiden.

"Uh, your honor, may I just—."

"No," the judge uttered sternly, and intolerantly. "And while I am speaking there will be no further interruptions."

In his inflexible and uncompromising demeanor judge Cedric Ambrose resumed where he left off.

"I am greatly horrified and sickened by what you have done— absolutely disgusted by it. The hurt, grief, and irreversible damage that you unnecessarily have caused to the family of these young victims is an atrocity. You ended the lives of those just beginning to live life and you took advantage of them sexually. Whether they consented is irrelevant. You had a responsibility, an obligation—not only as a man of God but as a decent human being. During this entire time, you have shown me no sign of remorse, just self-pity, like you are the victim. From the nature of your offenses, the irremediable impacts on the victims and their families, and the risk that you obviously pose to the community I am giving you a life sentence without parole upstate at *The Hollow Brook Penitentiary in Hollow Grove, New York* effective at once. Hopefully within that time you will genuinely find your way to God and to his forgiveness and transformation."

The tall, dark complexioned man in black cape, groomed pristine from the trim of his beard to the silky mat of his soft coiled black hair, brought his gavel down at the last call for attention, then uttered *"Court is adjourned."*

A tame roar of appeasement dominated the crowd of gatherers populated in the courtroom while the judge stepped from the bench to return to his chambers. Family and friends of the murdered students who had attended Saint Josephine Margaret Bakhita Preparatory and certain members of the community felt that justice served fair in the ruling.

*People hugged one another in a gesture of support and gratification.*

Kaiden Lucas's mother, father, aunt, and first cousin Alden Desmond watched him taken out of the courtroom in handcuffs lending encouraging words of love, consolation, and support.

The man's family did not excuse or by any means approve of what he had done though they knew and understood him while others did not. They knew him since he came into the world, and they knew the little wounded boy he once was and the individual he really was deep down inside from their relationships with him.

Esme Desmond, Alden's mother, and sister of Kaiden's mother Blythe, had mainly stuck through this ordeal to offer continual support for her sibling rather than for her nephew. Their children had grown up closely together during their youth to adulthood. They had still been tight up until this event.

Esme did not share the same sympathy or understanding for Kaiden as her sister and brother-in-law. She loved and remembered him for the person he once was but not for who he had become. Esme from her heart, mind, and soul could not bestow undying kindred loyalty to Kaiden that his parents unconditionally granted.

*Alden had a neutral perspective on the situation.*

He liked his cousin for who he had known him to be just like his mother had but he on the other hand did not condemn nor accept Kaiden with open arms. Alden remained aloof to the shock of what happened and distanced himself from the upheaval of it all. The instance was a complex one for him.

Nevertheless, he would not give Kaiden the cold shoulder if he ever decided to reach out to him from behind the walls of his dreary prison cell.

## Two

# A Time To Unwind

The *tonal* acoustic sounds of *soothing, energetic, rhythmic* popular music, which shifted in genre, *chorded salubriously* in the background while Alden Desmond sat at the bar with his best friend of seventeen years, Bryce Brandon.

*Nothing healed and relaxed like dining and fine music in an ambient setting of comforting food or refreshing drink.*

Thirty-two-year-old Bryce had stayed by Alden's side throughout the dilemma that concerned his cousin. Now that the ordeal had run its course and ended, they could move on from this nightmare altogether.

The female bartender placed two robust glass mugs of beer down in front of the men who had spent their long-drawn-out morning at a courthouse.

Alden dipped his upper lip into the frothy foam of the cold, sweet, bitter, rich, smokey, sharp flavor of malt liquor that had ascended to the surface to slightly flow over.

"*Ahhh,*" Alden interjected in exhilaration. *He then belched out a volume of gas.*

"Nothing like a cold one," Bryce agreed.

"Nothing like it!" Alden said, echoing his friend's words.

Amid the dimly lit small outspread of crowd that inhabited the pub Bryce had information to share.

"I have something to tell you, man."

Alden looked at his friend who had clear, smooth, pale ivory skin, a stubble beard, and auburn colored hair. "Yeah? What is it?" He asked, turning up another deep gulp of brew. His thick glass mug already halfway empty.

"I asked Yasmine to marry me yesterday. She said yes. We are going to get married."

Alden placed his empty glass to the counter of the table. His face seemed to have slightly fallen into disappointment. He wiped his mouth with the back of his hand then briefly gazed toward the mirror that dominated the wall behind the counter of the bar.

The medium built man of medium height and dark-brown eyes

did not appear thrilled to hear Bryce's latest bulletin.

Bryce saw the discontent that flashed upon Alden's face. He did not take the apathetic reaction to heart or interpret Alden's cold attitude as a form of jealousy. Bryce figured Alden felt they would see less of one another and not spend the time that they used to once he gotten married.

Alden was not the type to settle down. He played the field. He ran around with a different girl every week. Bryce had a monogamous relationship. He strictly dealt with one woman. During his lifetime he had never been a cheat or a womanizer.

# Three

## *Old Flame*

***Two Weeks Later***

Shortly after eleven am on a Saturday morning Bryce received a call from Alondra Delmira.

*He was shocked.*

Bryce had broken up with the woman three years ago. She had not taken the separation well and had given him hell before she finally let go of the one-sided relationship back then.

Bryce, barely awake when he answered the phone, met with instant jabber too loud and discursive to follow in such a rapid succession of words that had tirade from Alondra's outspoken, undiplomatic mouth.  Unable to calm his ex-girlfriend down enough to decipher whatever she tried to convey Bryce slammed the phone down on its cradle.

He wondered if Alondra had lost her mind as he stretched rising from the king size bed of his seventeen thousand dollar a month loft apartment in lower Manhattan. Bryce walked unsteady in his gait toward the bathroom still groggy from sleep.

He took a warm damp washcloth to wipe the crust from the corners of his eyes then brushed his teeth.

In the kitchen before he showered and prepared for work, he made a pot of coffee and an omelet. Bryce did not usually work on the weekend, but he had a deadline to meet. As a multimedia artist who worked for motion picture industries and in scientific settings, he currently aspired to become self-employed and about to leap out on his own in a month from now after this big project deal that he finished went through.

At the sink while he rinsed and dried dishes in his strikingly beautiful enormous size kitchen that had an industrial theme *backsplash* ornate with brick cladding, dark-wooden cabinets, and elegant ceiling track lights the phone rang for the second time this morning.

*Fully awake and on a full stomach Bryce answered with clarity and vibrancy.*

"Hello?" he said in his natural charming style of speech. "Bryce speaking."

"Bryce!"

*At once the man recognized the person on the other end of the line.*

"Look Alondra," he said firmly. "I—."

"No wait, Bryce," she said, cutting him off.

Calm and coherent in her address this time around he listened to what the woman had to say. Alondra sounded far from the highly agitated irrational person who maundered nonsensically.

Bryce later hung up the telephone miffed. Alondra still had strong feelings for him. She heard he had gotten engaged and the idea of him married to someone else drove her into a frenzy.

The jilted lover he fell out of love with hung on in hope of him one day hooking back up with her. She had left him alone in the three years that had passed, yet had not forgotten the passion they once shared, and she had not fallen out of love with him.

While Bryce committed himself to Yasmine, the new love of his life, he had to deal with the fact that Alondra *fervently* wanted *her man* back.

## Four

# A Bite To Eat

On Monday, Bryce met with Alden for lunch at *The Spicy Grille*, a place that served quality sirloin and exotic drinks.

The guys enjoyed a plush outside view of scenery at one of the bar tables aligned by the windows to the store front. Thick cuts of richly seasoned beef steak with baked and roasted potatoes steamed aromatically from their generously stacked plates.

"You know, Alondra called me over the weekend. She was upset because she knows I am getting married. She brought up how I never offered to marry her even when she had gotten pregnant. She even mentioned Yasmine. I do not know how she found out about our engagement."

Alden chewed on a decadent piece of meat then said, "I told her."

*Bryce was shocked.*

"You told her?!"

"Yeah," Alden uttered unconcerned as if the information that he volunteered to Bryce's ex was nothing serious.

*With a quick shake of the head and prolonged blink of the eyes Bryce did a figurative double-take at what he had just heard.*

"When? Where, how?" Bryce asked. "I am confused. Where and when did you run into Alondra and how did it come about that you felt the need to broadcast my business."

"It wasn't like that, man," Alden explained. "I saw her at the theater a week ago when I took Kerri out on Broadway to see that play that she kept raving about. She spotted me first and asked me how you were doing. I told her you are doing great in your career, that you are happy, and that you are getting married. I know I did not have to go there but I thought by telling her it would get her off your back for good. You know that little fatal attraction she had for you when you cut her loose. I could tell she is still carrying a torch for you. I was just looking out for your best interest."

Bruce ruminated on Alden's words. *He had a point.* From the conversation he had with Alondra over the phone on Saturday she had not gotten over him and moved on. Instead of Alden driving the woman further away he brought Alondra closer toward him. His strategy backfired and enkindled blind rage.

# Five

# Keeping A Tab On

Yasmine squinted in the luminescence of the sun. Her long, fine, straight, silky black hair flew wildly amid the sporadic winds. She stood picturesque on the boardwalk by the pier taking in breaths of fresh air.

Bryce stared into Yasmine's hypnotic brown eyes only to lose himself in them a thousand and one times more.

*The scent of her perfume, the touch of her skin, the warmth of her caress.*

Yasmine smelled of fresh white rose, she felt delicate as plush linen, she encompassed a gentleness beyond the captivation of an intimate embrace.

From a distance in a parked vehicle someone watched Bryce

take Yasmine passionately in his arms. They saw them *French kiss, fondle, cuddle, talk, smile,* and *laugh*—and the scene caused great distress in the coveting individual.

# Six

# Mail

Alden arrived home from his routine thirty-minute jog three days a week. He made a habit to run on *Mondays, Wednesdays,* and *Fridays.*

The thirty-one-year-old man drenched in sweat during this mild winter in *January* checked his mailbox before inserting the key inside the door to his fourth-floor two-bedroom *Manhattan* duplex that had a private outdoor terrace that showed wonderful midtown skyline views.

The man of medium height and build dropped his articles of mail to the coffee table near the decorative fireplace then headed to his renovated marble bathroom to refresh himself in the shower.

*He scrubbed his armpits, his chest, neck, back, between his butt cheeks, penis, testicles, scrotum, thighs, legs, and feet.*

Alden towel-dried his voluminous mat of dark brown freshly shampooed hair and patted down his moist pale ivory-colored skin.  He wrapped a large bath towel around his lower body after he threw the smaller damp towel inside the hamper and left from the domain of the washroom.

The heat that permeated throughout the apartment felt just as comfortable as a warm summer day.  Barefoot with his bare chest exposed he sauntered to the kitchen. Alden prepared a glass of gin on ice then went to the living room.

He turned on the television, settled on the couch, started to go over his mail when he saw an envelope addressed to him from The Hollow Brook Penitentiary in upstate Hollow Grove, New York.

# Seven

# Ardent Admirer: Letter One

Barefoot in a white tank top, and light-brown fleece shorts, in the loft of Bryce Brandon's apartment, Yasmine stood over the stove sauteing *thyme-spice* zucchini, and shrimp pasta with scallops.

The lean-figured woman with shapely pale olive-tone legs and a flat wide derriere had two flames going. She managed two nonstick stainless steel pans like the professional chef that she absolutely was not.

Though Yasmine did not have expert skills when it had come to cooking, she knew how to prepare a variety of healthy, decent meals when suited. Bryce had come and embraced Yasmine from behind. She smiled. He smiled. Then Bryce pecked his darling on the side of her neck.

After a tight squeeze and hug the man of medium height and medium build with medium-dark red hair released Yasmine from his grip to go check the mailbox. He had just awoken from a nap.

"Dinner will be ready in three minutes," Yasmine said in her soft-spoken voice.

*The couple had slept in late. They had been up all last night into the wee hours of the morning and did not go to bed until after eleven am.*

While Yasmine set the table in the dining area Bryce opened an anonymous letter addressed to him after he returned from the ride on the elevator. The note he removed from the envelope disturbed him.

**It read:**

*My Dear Bryce,*

*I saw you and her together the other day. The sight of you kissing her, holding her—made me want to explode. I do not even want to mention the thought of you having sex with her.*

*Break this relationship off Bryce. It will never work out. I am the one for you. Me and no one else.*

*Please Bryce, do not make me get her out of the way to take what is really mine. You and I have too much history together. I knew you before she ever came into the picture, and there is no room for her in our photo album. She cannot compare to the memories we share and that I look back on.*

*Truly Yours—Forever and always*

"Babe?!" Yasmine called for the fifth time. "Where are you? What are you doing? Come on, dinner is on the table."

Engulfed in the contents of the letter Bryce had not heard Yasmine beckon him. He had automatically tuned out. Quickly before she had come to look for him, and walk in on him while he held this note, Bryce placed the letter back inside the envelope and stuffed it between the pages of a book that occupied his elaborately sectioned bookshelf.

# Eight

# Family Ties

Bryce met Alden for their weekly get-together.  Today they occupied the billiard hall on the upper east side of Manhattan. While the men played a game of pool Alden spoke about a correspondence that he received.

"Bryce," Alden uttered solemnly, his dark eyes resigned.

"Yeah? What is up?" Bryce said. He heard the gravity in Alden's voice and saw a look of surrender dominate over his normally steadfast demeanor.

"I got a letter from Kaiden.  He wrote me from jail." Alden chuckled. "That probably sounded stupid. I mean where else would he write me from. It is not like he is ever going to get out."

Bryce sympathized. "I know it's hard."

"I still cannot believe all of this really happened. I never saw it coming with Kaiden. I feel sorry mostly of all for his parents who I need to visit. I have not seen them since the sentencing."

"How is your mother?" Bryce asked.

"She is fine a little too fine. It is like she does not care about Kaiden. I think inside she despises him for what he did. But how can I blame her? What he did was demonic."

Bryce shot a ball in a corner pocket then asked Alden, "What did Kaiden write in the letter?"

"He said that prison is a terrible place, a violent place. At the facility they placed him in a maximum-security unit because other inmates there had threatened his life."

"Oh, wow," Bryce said, ceasing from the game to join Alden in a moment of somber reflection.

Bryce decided this was not a proper time to mention the letter that he received.

**Nine**

# Conducting Business

Yasmine walked the floors in her dark green/mocha-brown/black suede suit-jacket and matching skirt. Tucked underneath the exquisitely designed skirt a mocha-brown, tie-neck, Bishop-sleeve blouse that coordinated flatteringly with the pair of dark-green suede pumps Yasmine wore on her feet.

The thirty-year old interior designer guided two clients through the rooms of their huge new three-level luxurious contemporary-modern home. The mother and daughter had turned to and hired Yasmine for her expert ability to fully utilize their interior space. They looked to have both functionality in the environment and beauty.

Trained in the use of lighting, color, furniture, and other aspects of decor Yasmine used software and rough sketches to create high quality designs to highlight and magnify their residential space.

Sought out by an extensive array of prospective customers and returning clients for her professionalism and outstanding artistry, Yasmine Luella made an impact in her rewarding field of work.

She expected to design plans and outlines for the home she and Bryce prepared to move into after their wedding. The couple were deciding whether to leave the state or to by a new home in another borough of New York. They had tired from living in the hustle and bustle of Manhattan—*while at a time they could not get enough of the excited activity and movement around the city*—they now sought out a quieter, calmer environment to settle down at.

*Yasmine's android clanged while in the middle of discourse with her clients.*

"Excuse me for a moment," Yasmine politely said to the enthusiastic mother and daughter enamored with the managing of their home. The women glanced around the areas of the place currently in development. Their faces lit, dominated with smiles, they admired the breathtaking interior work that had already started.

Yasmine gazed down at the screen of her mobile device. She saw a text from an unknown number.

**"I recommend that you leave Bryce now while you still have**

**time. Overall, you and he will never work out. He is mine. He belongs to me. You will never become his wife; I will make sure of it."**

*Of the message, Yasmine did not feel threatened or alarmed. She found the correspondence odd, and it had aroused her curiosity.*

She really did not know what to make of the text and the woman did not have the time currently anyhow. Yasmine put her phone away and resumed where she left off at during her meet there in the home.

# Ten

## Coming Clean

Yasmine did not see Bryce until a day after she received the cryptic anonymous text. She had not phoned him beforehand about it. She waited to see him in person before she mentioned the incident for discussion.

When the man read over the message, he confessed that he had received an item of mail similar in context to the text and that he had an idea of who had sent them.

Bryce explained the situation with his former girlfriend Alondra and how she had called him weeks ago still professing her love for him.

Disappointed that Bryce had not come to her earlier with this information the woman understood the position he felt placed in. He did not want to concern her with an unstable woman that he intended to manage on his own if or when things started to escalate.

Instead of acting on impulse or jumping ahead Bryce decided to deal with the situation as it developed rather than acting by assumption, or the possibilities, especially since circumstances tended to change.

Bryce also did not want to cause a disturbance to the genuine, beautiful, loving relationship he and Yasmine shared. They had a rare, once in a lifetime romance that most people never find or have.

While Yasmine dissatisfied with Bryce for not coming to her sooner about Alondra, she overlooked the matter. Yasmine did not have any trust issues with Bryce. She had complete faith in him, and she was secure within herself that is why she wished he had have treated her with that same trust and respect.

The trust that Yasmine did have in Bryce did not mean she did not think he could cheat she just did not believe that he would from the bond they had between them.

*Bryce was ultimately content with Yasmine. She was the love of his life. No other woman could compare to her in his eyes.*

**Eleven**

# Pleasant Surprise

A knock pounded from outside the door. *Then it happened again.*

When no one answered, the bell chimed incessantly. *"Okay! Okay!"* a voice bellowed as it raised high then low.

*The door opened. Their eyes met.*

Bryce glared at the green-eyed woman whose hair wrapped in a bath towel while a robe covered her thick, solid, medium-size body.

While she tied the belt to her lavish, embroidered, maroon-colored fleece bathrobe the perplexed individual stood speechless.

"We need to talk," Bryce said.

He politely barged his way in past the woman without coming off as violent or threatening.

She closed the door behind then asked, "Bryce what are you doing here? How did you find me?"

"I have my ways," said the man.

Bryce did a quick sweep of the apartment as he took in glances to prudently inspect his surroundings.

"Look, Alondra," he uttered firmly. "You have to stop this."

An expression of confusion dominated over Alondra's light-brown face. *And her reaction was genuine.*

"Stop what?"

*Bryce gave Alondra a derisive eye roll.* "Alondra, look. I did not come here to play games. You know exactly what."

The medium height man dressed in a white hoodie with a fashionable contrast-colored beige/white double-patch pocket reversible jacket and dark-brown pair of canvas pants removed the letter anonymously addressed to him.

Alondra saw Bryce reach into his back pocket to hand her a folded envelope with a note inside.

*The woman scanned the note carefully.*

"I did not write this," Alondra said.

"Oh, come on, Alondra! If you did not write the letter who else did?!"

*Bryce had lost his temper.*

*Alondra was now about to lose hers.*

She placed the letter back into the envelope and handed the correspondence back to Bryce.

He furrowed his thin brows, conflicted. *If Alondra was pretending to be oblivious to the situation, she did a rather decent job of doing so.*

"Okay now, you are not going to raise your voice at me here in my home.  You bombard your way in here unannounced, accusing me of something I know nothing about, you better get a hold of yourself. Now I do not know who wrote the letter. You should know me well enough to know that I am not the hide and seek type. Obviously, it must be another one of your past lovers that you jilted."

*Alondra laughed aloud.  She thought it good for him in return for how he dumped her.*

"You know me," Alondra said. She removed the towel from her head to let the damp mane of her thick, long, golden-brown hair to fall gracefully down past her shoulders. She then untied her robe to reveal the tender flesh of her nudity.

Bryce shielded his eyes from her indiscretion then headed toward the door to leave from the apartment.

"It was nice seeing you again, Bryce," Alondra uttered from behind. "I hope it won't be the last."

## Twelve

# Another Letter To Strike Curiosity

Yasmine entered her fiancé's humongous, stunning loft with the spare key he had made months ago. Welcomed to freely come and go from his apartment as she pleased, Yasmine fetched Bryce's mail from the mailbox on her way up in the elevator.

Fingering through the articles of mail Yasmine saw a letter addressed to Bryce from a *Kaiden Lucas* at *The Hollow Brook Penitentiary* in upstate *Hollow Grove, New York.*

Then it had come to her. *Kaiden Lucas,* formerly known as *Father Asher Verlice,* was the first cousin of Bryce's best friend Alden. But why was he writing to Bryce?

# Thirteen

# Kaiden

Tears streamed from Alden Desmond's dark-brown eyes as he sat with Bryce Brandon at *The Bean Roastery Coffee* and *Pastry Shop*.

Bryce comforted his friend after having found out that his cousin Kaiden hung dead in his jail cell a night ago from a clear suicide.

"I had just visited him at the prison," Alden said. "I know that he did not kill himself. Someone else did that. It was an inside job. They made it look like he killed himself."

*Though Alden appeared highly upset and emotional in his grief the man's notion sounded plausible to Bryce.*

A notification alert emitted from Bryce's mobile device. There was a text message from Yasmine.

"That is odd," Bryce said aloud. "Yasmine just texted me. She said I received a letter in the mail from Kaiden."

Alden raised his head, startled. He wiped his eyes and tried to collect himself.

"She said you received a letter from Kaiden?"

"Yeah," Bryce said, nodding his head.

# Fourteen

# The Loft

Someone buzzed the intercom to the loft from the main door to the street of the upper-class neighborhood in lower Manhattan.

Yasmine spoke through the two-way electrical device attached to a wall inside the industrial-style, luxury, palace-like apartment.

"I have a delivery package," spoke a female voice.

Yasmine pressed the button to the intercom that opened the main level door. When the freight elevator rose to the floor of the loft, she slid open the custom steel doors, bewildered. This was no delivery person who stood in front of Yasmine—though the individual did arm herself with a fancily wrapped package.

A strikingly gorgeous woman wearing a full-length fox fur

coat walked through the entrance. The woman in a chic fusion of grayish-silver and black shaded garment smelled of delicious, sweet perfume and she glimmered modestly in dazzling expensive jewels.

"Excuse me. Who are you and how may I help you?" Yasmine asked, a bit overwhelmed and taken aback by this high-class-looking *stranger/intruder*.

"My name is Alondra. *Alondra Lumet.*"

In a slight bow of the head with erect eyes, Yasmine uttered in validation, "Bryce's ex-girlfriend, Alondra?"

"Yes. That is the one," Alondra uttered confidently, her radiant green eyes scrutinizing every aspect of the place she took hold of.

Bryce had not mentioned how beautiful this woman was and how well-to-do she appeared. He just made it seem as if Alondra was a little unhinged and needy which looked quite the opposite through her discerning eyes. Yasmine wondered what else Bryce had withheld when it had come to Alondra.

"Here," Alondra said, handing Yasmine a generous size gift-wrapped package she had picked up at Bloomindale's on 59th Street and Lexington Avenue. "It is an early wedding present from me to you."

"Why are you harassing us?" Yasmine asked. It is over between you and Bryce."

"I am not harassing either of you. And for the record, darling. It will never be over between me and Bryce—not for me anyway."

"What are you doing here then? And why did you send those written addresses to Bryce and me. He received a letter, and I, a text."

"Bryce came to see me this morning. I had nothing to do with any letter or text. I told him that."

"He did not tell me he came to see you."

"What else is he not telling you?"

Yasmine gazed at this woman with soft, taut, silky light-brown skin, thick lustrous golden-brown hair, and a magnificent figure underneath that unbuttoned posh coat. "From the looks of you why are you still hung up on Bryce. I am sure you could have a selective choice of available suitors."

"It is not about who I can have. It is about who I want. But obviously Bryce does not want me anymore, and he never will. I realized that this morning after he left my apartment. I just had to see to whom I lost him."

*The buzzer to the intercom to the main door sounded.*

Yasmine spoke through the speaker of the device.

"Hi Yasmine—."

Right away, Yasmine recognized the voice. "I am buzzing you up right now," she said.

*Yasmine had interjected abruptly.* Enthusiasm gushed the moment she heard the voice of a familiar acquaintance. Yasmine glad she was no longer alone in the company of this Alondra woman whom she did not trust.

A half hour to forty-five minutes later Bryce rode the elevator up to the loft. The man overtaxed and tired. All he wanted to do was shower, eat, watch a little television, then go to sleep. It had been hours since he left from the coffee shop and went his own separate way from Alden.

*Personal and professional commitments depleted extensive periods of time for them these days. The two men both had returned to their usual functions and obligations. They had responsibility to uphold in their careers, at their workplaces, and at their homes.*

The social meetings they planned weekly gave them an outlet. Alden and Bryce stayed the best of friends as the two made space for one another to connect.

When Bryce reached the entrance of the apartment something appeared a bit off. In the distance of the large-size room Yasmine lay upon the floor.

"Yasmine?" Bryce called, endearingly.

*The woman did not reply.*

Bryce doubted Yasmine fell asleep on the floor, not as affluently embellished as his apartment was, it just did not make sense.

He walked over in the direction to where his fiancé lay positioned. Yasmine faceward on her back appeared lifeless. Bryce saw where blood had trickled from her nose and he took the woman in his embrace, lifting her medium limp body from the hard, glazed flooring of the loft.

*Tears fell from Bryce's dejected brown eyes when he realized the love of his life was dead.*

A letter with drops of blood smeared on the surface rested placed atop Yasmine's body. The handwritten note written in unusual handwriting—to throw one off he assumed— slid to the floor when Bryce grabbed the body. Looking down at the letter Bryce stooped to pick up the piece of paper, and he read it.

"I warned you to get rid of her. She stood in the way of us being together. I had to do it. I am tired of waiting. I have already waited too long for you."

*A noise came from behind one of the sofas.*

Startled, Bryce raised to his feet to look around. He heard a moan then a groan like that of someone in pain.

He was not alone there in his loft. Someone else occupied the place besides him and his deceased fiancé.

"Who is there?"

The moan and groan had come again as the sounds of one trying to rise to their feet took hold. Bryce heard what sound like high-heeled shoes. He smelled the scent of strong perfume.

Then from behind a sofa trying to balance on her feet appeared Alondra. She wore a gray/silver/black fur coat spotted with blood.

Bryce did not have time to think he just reacted.

He charged at Alondra who was dazed and confused from a blow she had taken to the head.

*"You killed her! You killed her!"* Bryce shouted in blind rage.

Alondra in need of medical care and barely able to stand on her feet tried to signal Bryce for help and warning but he did not listen. Sharp, dull pain jabbed and throbbed from the back of her head. The room slightly spun and Alondra too vulnerable to defend herself had become victim to Bryce's uncontrollable rage and fury. Alondra died in the grips of his unclenching hands.

Bryce strangled Alondra to death.

The heartbroken man with auburn hair and brown eyes let out an awful howl of despair and burst heavily into tears, once again.

He staggered over to Yasmine's body to kiss and hold her in his arms. While he held the dead corpse of his fiancé in his embrace a deep voice spoke to him from behind.

"The wait is over. And I have waited for this moment. We can finally be together. No more women between us. Just you and me."

Bryce in a state of hurt, shock, and bewilderment recognized the voice from behind. His glassy eyes turned around to see his best friend Alden there in the large room of his loft. Alden had been there waiting for him since he left the coffee shop hours ago.

He had arrived earlier while Alondra was about to leave. He had killed Yasmine after she buzzed him up to the floor. Then bludgeoned Alondra with a metal pipe. He thought he had killed her too until she had just come to.

Alden had appeared from Bryce's bedroom with nothing on but one of Yasmine's translucent peach-colored negligees.

Covered in sweat, violently glaring into the twisted eyes of his longtime friend, Bryce sat on the verge of going into overdrive. Alden's torrid voice and the words that spew forth had galvanized the man into action. *Speechless and immobile in the moment, yet only a matter of seconds before he broke wild.*

# The Dollhouse

# The Arrival

"Lorna!" her mother called from downstairs. Your boxes have arrived!"

Twelve-year-old Lorna Ferguson appeared from the sheets of her aesthetically draped canopy bed, excited.

*It is here!*

The brown complexioned girl with comely onyx-colored eyes slipped her feet in her fluffy white bunny slippers to rush down the staircase in her pajamas.

Cordelia Ferguson kneed the largest of the three boxes that had come with the support of her arms.

The attractive-looking lady with soft, firm dark skin, thick straight shoulder length black hair, and exquisite nut-brown eyes lifted the two smaller boxes over to the side away from the door.

The sterling mother of three watched Lorna zoom down the steps to the foyer of their five-bedroom modern farmhouse-style home found in *Bayberry Hills* of *Hickory Creek, New York.*

"What did you order?" Cordelia asked. The large box seemed to weigh a ton.

"A dollhouse and accessories," Lorna said going to inspect the boxes that address labels bared her name.

Uncle Brooks had gifted Lorna two hundred dollars for her twelfth birthday a week ago. She had surfed the internet to a site called *Mystic Enchants.* A beguiling webpage for *New Age* products that dealt in the esoteric.

*Special* and *different* since birth Lorna by nature was drawn to the arcane and sibylline, and she had a fascination for the otherworldly.

*At the age of twelve Lorna still loved to play with barbies and life-like doll figures.*

# The Set Up

By afternoon during this bright, cloudless day of late spring Lorna had fully assembled the three-floor dollhouse— that stood just as tall as she did—and organized its furniture, and people accessories.

Cordelia entered the room and marveled.

"Oh, my." she said, her thick lips in a shade of red, opened-wide in pleasant surprise. "That dollhouse is beautiful. I have never seen one like it. And look at the cute rooms—and that furniture. They did not have a toy and features like this when I was a kid, though we did have great stuff. You are lucky to have found an item like this. Nowadays toys are of mediocre quality in comparison to when I came up."

Lorna smiled. She held doll-people in her hands while at play in the sections of the color-coordinated dollhouse.

Cordelia's eyes shifted to the bluish to reddish-purple sparkly item that sat on the desk to the wooden bone-white *Vanity*. The article looked like an odd cluster of sliced watermelon.

"What is this, Lorna?"

Lorna turned her head to see what her mother referred to.

"That is an Amethyst."

"Oh," Cordelia uttered, in realization. "As in Amethyst gemstone?"

"Yes mom," Lorna said, her face buried back inside the dollhouse.

The slender woman of medium height went to further glance at the object she had not seen up close before in its natural form. Used to seeing amethyst quartz designed in fashionable jewelry she had not come close to seeing the crystals in the raw, and partly attached to its rock/geode.

The violet stone sat prettily and seemed to exude an energy throughout the room now that she had become aware of its presence.

*Cordelia left the room shaking her head and wondering what her young daughter was into.*

The smart, advanced girl Lorna was, always led by spirit to know and to learn, she had become aware of the properties the amethyst owned. She intended to provoke and enhance a personal transformation, balance, healing of her body, mind, and soul, along with inner peace and healing overall.

Lorna had suffered a terrible accident two years ago that had killed her grandparents and left her partially paralyzed for ten months. While Lorna regained mobility in her legs, they would give out from time to time, and she walked with a slight limp.

*A nerve in the legs damaged, in one of the limbs severe than the other, the doctor had informed Lorna had to eventually undergo another surgery in the future to prevent deadening of the nerves where she would become permanently paralyzed.*

Lorna sporadically experienced pain in her upper thighs and lower legs, yet she was able to run and get around like a normal twelve-year-old to a limit.

*The amethyst— no problem!* But thank goodness her mother did not notice the other two items of material she had bought to attract the energy of the things she wanted.

The first day of *Summer* had begun last week. Lorna anxious for school to let out sat at an outside lunch table unwrapping foil from the *roast turkey*, *cheese*, *lettuce*, and *tomato* sandwich Cordelia prepared for her this morning before she left the house.

Oversize bully Kyra Harris walked over to Lorna. She demanded the girl twice her size to hand over the sandwich.

Unafraid, Lorna ignored the pug-faced, *nappy-haired* nuisance who had a matted, woolly-textured *birds-nest* as an excuse for a mane.

The bold lass with striking dark eyes and thick straight black hair that hung just past her shoulders, grabbed the sliced in half turkey and cheese betwixt toasted bread and brought it up to her mouth.

When Lorna took a bite of her food Krya furiously slapped it from her mouth out of her hand.

*A heated fight broke out.*

Lorna lost her balance in the grapple and Kyra took advantage of the opportunity by picking up and slamming the medium size rubber utility trash basket that perched nearby over the girl's delicate bare legs.

The twelve-year-old who had worn a skirt on this last day of the school term bellowed out a penetrating sound of anguish. She lingered on the concrete ground of the schoolyard, turned over to the side, drawing the attention of those who solicitously flocked in her direction.

# Bound

Lorna spent the first two weeks of summer recess cooped up in the seat of a wheelchair. A physical and occupational therapist visited the young lady when she no longer needed the chair but needed the use of a two-wheel walker inside the house and a four-wheel one for outdoor use.

*Oh, how Lorna hated Kyra Harris. The overgrown doofus had made her legs worse.*

During the days she sat hampered from doing the things she loved Lorna surfed the web to revisit the *Mystic Enchants* website. At the navigation menu she clicked on people doll-figures to add to her dollhouse collection. She added two novel items to her cart and received a confirmation that the order would ship in four to five business days.

The unopened package from the delivery had sat atop a bureau in the bedroom. Now that she was out the wheelchair, less depressed, and flexible with her limbs Lorna fetched the contents from *Mystic Enchants* whose company headquartered over in the next county of *Boulder Pines, New York.*

On one of the new doll-figures Lorna dabbed a pinch of oil she had bought from the first order placed with the dollhouse a month ago. She then wrote the initials of *Kyra Harris* behind the doll.

*"Lorna!"* Cordelia called. *"Time for dinner!"*

Lorna ceased from her activity. She idly laid the doll atop the roof of the dollhouse until after dinner. She then would resume the unfinished work of imagination once she later returned.

While the family of four sat at the dinner table *Spike*, the family beagle, hung under the table waiting for anyone to drop down scraps. *Koja*, the family's gorgeous long-haired, silky coated, chocolate-point, blue-eyed *Birman* cat paced and sprinted around the carpeted floors of the home.

She climbed the steps to the curved staircase then wandered aimlessly in the domain of Lorna's finely adorned bedroom. Clawing from here to there *Koja* jumped to the top of the dollhouse to fortuitously knock the doll figure Lorna had left on the roof of her *splendidly crafted dollhouse.*

The doll fell and rolled somewhere out of site but later found its way into the sharp teeth of *Koja's* mouth as she took the toy to one of her unknown hiding places within the home.

# Quality Time

When dinner ended Lorna wanted to go to her bedroom to finish what she started. Her father and mother convinced her to sit with them in the family room for a movie.

Lorna's parents felt that she spent too much time in that room lately so soon after the recovery from her limbs that already had prior injury to them.

Hadlee, the eldest of the children, and Lorna's big sister, had a date with friends this evening.

"In no later than ten," Zachary told his daughter.

"Sure thing, dad!" the seventeen-year-old uttered in her step out the door from the kitchen that led to the outside of the house.

Hadlee had a habit of coming home far after curfew.

Eight-year-old Elliot joined Lorna and their parents for a

comedy flick highlighted with bowls of freshly air popped popcorn drizzled in hot melted butter.

# Where Are You?

One movie turned into three viewed flicks among the family during quality time well-spent in their unfaltering modes of bonding. The night had turned out a delightful, enjoyable one for Lorna, grateful to her parents for persuading a change of pace, the young one met an uplift in spirits.

By eleven-thirteen Lorna had forgotten all about the doll-figure and the intention behind the activity she had begun. It could wait until the morning. Right now, she wanted to crawl into bed and sleep soundly. Lorna was exhausted.

In the morning Lorna looked high and low to no avail for the toy figure she left atop the dollhouse.

*Where could it have gone?*

After a prolonged fruitless search Lorna gave up. The idea of Koja roaming around in her room to seize the doll never once crossed Lorna's puzzled mind.

Lorna went over to the dollhouse to play. Hadlee peeked inside the bedroom on her walk down the hall.

"You are too old to still play with dolls. Why don't you grow up—get a boyfriend or something—you freak," The tall, dark complexioned, teenager with large uneven breast and a huge derriere uttered, vitriolically.

Lorna rolled her eyes while her back faced her sister. Hadlee talked so nasty toward her at times and was often overly critical for no reason. Cordelia explained in the past that Hadlee was just jealous of her because she was not out doing the same things Hadlee had done when she was twelve.

Though Cordelia emphasized to Lorna to pay Hadlee no attention, because as a young girl she was on the right path, Hadlee still had a way to get under her skin.

While Lorna sat on the carpeted floor across from her beloved dollhouse she held a female people-figure in her hand dangling it with her fingers by the mini steps of the toy house.

In a mild fit of anger incited by her sister's unkind words Lorna hit the figure against the mid stairway structure and let the doll fall on its plastic mold along the patterned slope downward.

*Concomitantly, a loud scream rang out, followed by a heavy thump.*

The shriek that turned into piercing howls and wails echoed horridly from the hallway to the Ferguson home.

Hadlee had fallen down the steps and broken her hip.

*She had also broken her jaw when her face smashed into the banister on her way down.*

# Pleasant Bewitching Changes

While Hadlee Ferguson's teenage life had slowed down due to the injury to her hip and jaw—unable to currently walk and unable to talk—Lorna's ailments seemed to have greatly improved without explanation to the doctors.

It guessed that she no longer needed future surgery to correct the nerve damage to her limbs.

Not only did her physical mobility enhance but her environment at home too. Lorna doubted she would receive any more verbal abuse or harsh criticism from her sister for being a so-called *goody two shoes*.

Now that Hadlee had to stay put Lorna also doubted belittlement inwardly by her sister for not running the street as she once did when she could. A lesson learned for her mocking Lorna playing with dolls. Now Hadlee had no choice but to *play victim* at home by herself.

What mystified the doctors, and her parents, was of no mystery for Lorna. She knew the power of the *Amethyst* as a protective stone in her benefit.  She also knew the power of the other magical items ordered from *Mystic Enchants* once they had fused with her natural magical endowments that she learned she had from the age of five.

*The energy in vibration had absolutely brought to her personal transformation, balance, healing of her body/mind and soul, and inner peace.  Lorna noticed spiritual awareness come upon her, a magnified psychic ability, balance, and relief in stress helped by meditation and communication with her spirit guide.*

# Summer Day

On the back porch inside the outdoor patio Zachary barbecued franks and hamburgers.  Lorna sat at the black oval-shaped cast aluminum framed table that accented a scrolled floral design with matching cushioned chairs drinking a cold glass of lemonade.

*"Daddy,"* she said.

"Yes, sweetheart?" Her father answered.

"Now that I am healing, and my legs are stronger I was thinking about taking swimming lessons. I want to one day become a scuba diver and would like to start training now."

*Turning over a hamburger, Zach was not too keen on the idea, he shook his head unsure.*

"I don't know, Lorna. I do not like the idea of you going into the water. You are just starting to show incredible improvement in your body. It is still soon. Do you know the people who drown a year without physical issues? You are not in the clear just yet. Let the doctors continue to run tests and see how your body responds and builds with the therapy exercise sessions they are sending you to. If you still feel you want to train for the water in a year, then I will give it serious thought. In the meantime, my answer is no."

"Dad!" Lorna tried to persuade. "I really do not need these exercise sessions. I have healed. How long do I have to stay stuck visiting doctors and going to therapy?! You all treat me like I am a disabled!"

"Nonsense," Zachary uttered. "Lorna, we love you. We are just looking out for you and your well-being. What has gotten into you? Do you realize how close you came to not ever walking again? Yes, you have recently—beyond my understanding and everyone else's considering the circumstances you were under—made an outstanding improvement. However, Lorna, we cannot jump into things. We must take it slow to make sure you are out of the woods."

*Dissatisfied with her father's words Lorna stormed from the patio up to her room. Instead of acknowledging and accepting the logic and reason in Zachary's speech the twelve-year-old behaved as the immature brat that she ordinarily was not.*

She kneeled to the floor by her dollhouse and grabbed a male people-figure.

"What was that about?" Cordelia asked her husband. *Lorna had hurled by her mother with such vehemence she had almost knocked her down.* Cordelia had brought out a tray of boiled corn on the cob to briefly roll on the grill for a smoky, delicious taste.

While Zachary went to share what needlessly sent Lorna into upset, he suddenly in an instant caught on flames. A peculiar eruption from the grill caused Zachary to rapidly catch on fire.

*Cordelia screamed, horrified.*

In a panic the woman ran for the garden hose as she shouted for eight-year-old Elliot to call 911. Hadlee, in no position to do anything, sat in her wheelchair on the patio shocked and mortified. Her father burned and all she could do was sit there and watch.

The event was traumatizing.

# What Is In This House That Is Coming From The House?

A week had passed, and Zachary Ferguson laid in a hospital at *County Brook Medical* clinging to life.

On the phone with a neighborhood friend who lived close-by Cordelia heard other disturbing news beside that of her husband from the woman who spoke on the other end of the line.

"Wow. First Tamia Harris and now you."

"What do you mean?" Cordelia asked.

"You mean, you didn't hear about it?" the woman said, thinking it had gotten around to everyone in Bayberry Hills.

"Hear what?"

"Tamia's daughter Kyra. The bully who harassed Lorna at school.

Savagely attacked and killed by a mountain lion on a family trip to Colorado weeks ago."

As her friend Linda told the story over the phone *Koja* had come up to Cordelia with a miniature toy doll in her mouth.

*What is this? she ruminated.*

Pensive, and distracted, Cordelia abruptly ended the discussion with her friend. She hung up the phone promising to return a call later after she checked something out.

Cordelia bent down and removed the object resembling an item from Lorna's dollhouse collection. The plastic mold now marred by teeth marks had the initials *K* and *H* written behind it.

The thirty-five-year-old woman just hit with an ominous, eerie, gut-feeling headed upstairs to her middle-child's room. Lorna was at an afternoon therapy exercise session.

The dark-complexioned woman of slender build and medium height walked over to the dollhouse and saw something unsettling.

Cordelia saw that the cardboard in the section of one of the dollhouse rooms had a thick, black patch of burnt matter upon the wall. Down below on the floor of the toy house was a people-figure half-charred. Beside the partially burned doll was a matchstick.

Another people-figure on the second floor of the dollhouse bent at the hip and indented at the mouth.

The woman with nut-brown colored eyes stood discomposed. *Was this art imitating life or was life imitating art?* This was the impossible that had seemed somehow to become possible. *Cordelia, mortified at the thought, while momentarily questioning her sanity.*

Reality made the woman face the unnerving, unbelievable truth.

*Hadlee had a severely altered mouth and hip that resemble one of Lorna's dolls. Zachary severely burned like another of the dolls. Kyra Harris, she found out viciously attacked by a Puma wildcat the tragedy enigmatically mimicked by the teeth-marked doll-figure in the jaw-grips of her harmless house cat.*

A car door slammed from the street in front of the house. The cab had dropped Lorna off from therapy.

Cordelia panicked looking around the room. Then the thirty-five-year-old woman of three noticed something else strange and darn near frightening there with her in the room.

Footsteps climbed the curved staircase to the Ferguson home. Lorna had gotten inside with the spare house key hidden underneath the welcome mat outside the main entrance to the home.

"*Mother,*" Lorna said when she reached the opened door to her bedroom.

*I am in the doghouse now*, Cordelia thought to herself, profoundly afraid of her twelve-year-old child.

"No mother," Lorna said, reading her mother's mind. *"You're in the dollhouse now, and you're not getting out."*

# Also by LaToya Lawrence

I am a natural-born writer who has written since childhood.

**New York Style Tales Of Suspense**
Three short stories that include thrills in a mixture of fictional towns around New York.

New York Style: Tales of Suspense Tantalizing Excitement in The City! – Join this two hundred sixty-five-page psychological thrill ride of murder, mystery, suspense, a bit of the supernatural, and fun!

Three short stories that include thrills in a mixture of fictional towns around New York.

## Tale one: Two Of A Kind

*Is Blood thicker than murder?*

*There is a secret buried deep in the soil of Cherry Hill. In a town of beautiful cities, lakes, and villages where trees grow tall, flowers bloom free, and the neighbors are friendly.*

*Is there an uncovered truth rising upon the surface? One of cruelness among rebellious youth? Or could it just be a hereditary factor where bloodline goes bad, and murder goes right.*

Mysterious murders take place in the lovely upscale town of Cherry Hills throughout Pennington, New York—killings and deaths that shock and bewilder residents in a city where scandalous crimes run sparse. There had not been such incident since the highly publicized murders that took place in early winter of January 1981 on Oakwood St. in the home of Evelyn and Ryan Barker.

**Tale two: The Lovers**

*What is it that is masquerading as ordinary, lurking brazenly on forbidden territory? Is there a price for playing with magic or is magic worth paying the price for?*

*Deep in the city streets of Manhattan lies a place for those who want to take a gamble at chance.*

*One may get lucky, or one may lose out.*

*In any fashion, delving in, one must accept the consequence that what was bought cannot be returned as there is no way to buy back what was once sold.*

*It is not wise to mess with things that are considered taboo as what is taboo can come back around to mess with you.*

A young man consults a voodoo priest and gets more than he bargains for when he takes home a personalized spell-kit, and all goes wrong.

**Tale three: Summer Fling**

*In a world of their own craziness, impulse, and greed, do you really know who the people around you are when they do not even know and cannot trust themselves?*

*Riding on a rollercoaster they cannot function to get off of—continuously spinning around only to come to nowhere to get them back to their sphere.*

*Dealing with them is enough to drive one crazy but a little craziness allows one to deal with the drive to survive.*

A successful woman takes a setback to bounce back in her career even stronger than ever before— inciting unknown events from the past of those around her to reveal mind-boggling secrets and mysteries that result in a multiple chain of unexpected murders.

www.ingramcontent.com/pod-product-compliance
Lightning Source LLC
Chambersburg PA
CBHW020644160726
47991CB00003B/1016